RIVER THAMES

LITTLE TOOT
ON THE THAMES

LITTLE TOOT

ON THE THAMES

BY
HARDIE GRAMATKY

G. P. Putnam's Sons   New York

Other books by Hardie Gramatky:

LITTLE TOOT

HERCULES

LOOPY

CREEPER'S JEEP

SPARKY

HOMER AND THE CIRCUS TRAIN

BOLIVAR

NIKOS AND THE SEA GOD

In a busy harbor, there lives a tugboat known as Little Toot. He is a friendly tug with a cheerful whistle, but he is very small.

He is too small to do the work of other tugs. They work hard all day pushing and shoving big boats about, while Little Toot never gets a chance.

Well, one day Little Toot decided he would try to tow a boat all by himself.

With no one to stop him, he ventured far out
to sea. There he caught the towline of a tramp
steamer. Then he began to tow. He pulled and
pulled with all his strength. He pulled until he
was blue in the face.

But alas! Poor Little Toot! He didn't
know much about towing. All the while he
thought he was towing the tramp steamer

the tramp steamer was towing him.

And across the wide ocean, too.

It was bound to end badly. And it did! When they reached a distant shore the tramp steamer just abandoned the little tug.

All alone in a strange world,
Little Toot had only one thought
— how to get home again.

It was a gray foggy world,
and the little tug didn't know
which way to turn. Instead, he sat
there in silence. His large round
smoke balls billowed up into the
fog like dumplings in a thick stew.

Sadly he thought of home. He thought of his father, Big Toot, and of Grandfather Toot and of all his friends. He wondered if ever he would see them again.

Out of the fog two eyes twinkled dimly through the mist. They belonged to an old barge Little Toot began to see. It was a Thames River barge, a rare vessel, but one he had heard about many times.

With a voice like a foghorn, the old barge said, "Use your hooter in the fog, or you may find yourself in a muddle!"

Little Toot did not know what a "hooter" was. Then he remembered he wasn't at home. A hooter must be a horn.

"If you want to go back to your home," the old barge told him, "you'll have to go see the queen. She can help you get home."

That was a good idea!

With a stout heart Little Toot set out on his journey to find the queen. The old barge pointed the way through the mist.

Little Toot had to peer carefully before him.
Who knew what strange things might be
lurking ahead? The fog gradually lifted, and
weird shapes began to appear. Mechanical
monsters with long scrawny arms rose up from
the edge of the river. Docks and wharves
creaked amid chugging sounds, and Little Toot
heard the rattle of chains.

Before he knew what was happening, he was entirely surrounded by monsters, their long arms reaching skyward. Some were loading cargo from barges into freighters and some were unloading cargo from freighters into barges. It was a busy place. And all the while a tough gang of tugs pushed and shoved their way into the confusion. They paid no attention to a greenhorn like Little Toot.

He wasn't wanted there. And Little Toot saw a good reason why. A brilliant red barge flying a danger flag was being loaded with explosives. It was enough to frighten anyone.

Little Toot threaded his way between cables and towlines in a frantic effort to get away. He hoped never to see this place again.

At last he was free!

The sun had cut through the haze; and there before him stretched a bridge with towers. It must be a gateway to somewhere, thought Little Toot. Since its drawbridge was already drawn, the little tugboat quickly slipped through.

Little Toot knew he was heading in the right direction, because it was beginning to be a beautiful world. Soon he must look for the queen.

Tooting past a castle on his right, he felt bolder and more himself again.

Then he came to London
Bridge — the best-known
bridge in the world. Gay
crowds passed overhead and
tossed him friendly
greetings.

Even the boats on the river towing their barges upstream seemed in a holiday mood as they jostled each other joyfully.

Little Toot thought it
must be a holiday, for along
the embankment marched a
group of grenadiers, as
sturdy and straight as a set
of tin soldiers.

Then came the Horse Guards. And then a golden coach! Wide-eyed in amazement, Little Toot bounced cheerfully along. It was like being in a real-life fairy tale.

It was pretty wonderful, too, for a little tug that was used to seeing only docks and wharves. He forgot entirely about going home.

He had time for a number of things and there was still so much to explore.

Much farther along, the river dwindled in size. Grass grew green along its banks.

Rounding a bend, Little Toot came upon a gay crowd. There were dinghies and punts and pleasure boats, all having a happy time.

But Little Toot was sure he was welcome.

He joined in the fun. The boats went around and around. Small ones and large ones, they all went around. Bagpipes squealed and trumpets blared. Boats swished up water and splashed each other and they all had a merry old time.

Little Toot was having such a
merry time that he never even saw
the pleasure boats stop playing.
They had all pulled to the side of
the river.

Poor Little Toot! He was right
in the middle of the boat-race
course and three racing boats were
headed his way.

No one thought to tell Little
Toot he was in the way. Instead,
the happy little tug went right on
circling about, until without
thinking he had formed a large
figure 8 in the river.

To make things even worse, he
was followed by a group of swans.

And the figure 8 took up
most of the river. There was
no room at all for the racing
boats to pass.

Boats and swans and crewmen all wound up in a hullabaloo.

That did it!

Little Toot was in terrible disgrace and everyone told him to go home.

He only wished he *could* go home. He longed to be home again. Now it was too late for anything, and there was no one to whom he could turn.

Suddenly, out of the shadows of the river came a familiar voice calling his name. It was a sound he would know anywhere.

There lying alongside a wharf was the old tramp steamer. He was all steamed up for a voyage, yet he was unable to move away from the dock.

"Grab a towline, pal, and help me get out of here," he said in a friendly voice. "I'll see that you get home if you do."

Little Toot was overjoyed at the thought of going home. Eagerly, he made fast to the towline and began to pull.

Slowly they moved away from the wharf.

Now, picking his way
among barges and lighters,
Little Toot towed and
steered carefully. He was
careful, too, not to awaken
the tough old tugs. No
telling what they would do
if aroused.

But it was the tramp steamer Little Toot should have worried about. Now that the old villain no longer needed help, he rudely shoved the little tugboat aside. Then, showing his true colors, he headed for the open river without so much as a thank-you.

As luck would have it, he got tangled in the lines of a barge. It was the red barge, too, and still flying the danger flag.

The barge was dragged into midstream. There it caught in a swift current, tore loose from the tramp steamer and capsized.

The old tramp headed downriver with hardly a backward glance.

The dangerous barge sank
without a sound.

It was a dreadful thing to
happen. Any seaman worth his salt
would know what a disaster to
river traffic this could be.

Little Toot knew what he had
to do.

Through the long night he stood guard over the sunken barge. The small red light on his portside blinked on and off like a channel marker, keeping ships at a distance.

When dawn broke over London, Little Toot was still at his post, almost too tired to move.

Suddenly, bells from Big Ben began to ring. Flags went up on Tower Bridge. This heralded a great celebration.

"The celebration is sure to be here on the Thames," Little Toot thought. "And the sunken barge is right in the way."

Frantically, the little tugboat sent up a volley of smoke balls. Frantically, he tooted his whistle. But try hard as he would, he could attract the attention of no one.

Something had to be done right away!

There was only one way of getting attention, but Little Toot shuddered to think of it. It had always gotten him into trouble before. Still, he had to take the chance.

With a burst of speed the little tugboat shot out across the river, circled back around by the sunken barge, and completed a large figure 8.

In no time at all fireboats and river police came scurrying, and with sirens screaming.

The sunken barge was raised and carefully hauled away.

Then downstream came a gallant procession of boats.

Leading the flotilla was none other than the Royal Barge.

It was a great celebration!
And after it was all over, Little
Toot was given a fine ovation.
Even the tough old tugs joined in
with a rollicking cheer.

Then Little Toot got his wish to go home.
And true to the prediction of the old Thames
River barge, it was the "queen" who helped him.

For the good ship *Queen Elizabeth* herself
escorted him all the way.

About the Author

HARDIE GRAMATKY created a juvenile classic when he wrote and illustrated *Little Toot*, published in 1939. He has since done eight other delightful books for children. Mr. Gramatky is equally famous for his fine arts, having won over thirty top watercolor awards. His paintings hang in permanent collections of many museums.

Little Toot has had a variety of honors. Among them: he has been a prizewinning float in the Pasadena Tournament of Roses; he has been made into a movie by Walt Disney; he has been translated into many languages, including Thai for the children of Thailand. Little Toot has been given away as a family-size boat on the Garry Moore television show; and all bookmobiles serving the Los Angeles area are named "Little Toot."